A tale of woodland enchant:

THE BLUEBELL FAIRY

Written and illustrated by Michelle A. Soden-Gilkes

Copyright ©2015 Michelle Anne Soden-Gilkes All rights reserved.
ISBN-10:1507701144   ISBN-13:978-1507701140
CREATESPACE PUBLISHING PLATFORM

First published January 2014 in Do You Believe In Magic by Michelle Anne Soden-Gilkes.

*For Aimee, who inspired me to write this book;
for Charlotte, who motivated me to finish it;
and for all the daydreamers
walking through Christmas Common in Maytime.*

This is the story of the bluebell fairy. Her job was to paint all the bluebell flowers in the wood. Now most people might think that bluebells naturally flower with blue blooms; actually they flower white, which is why very rarely you might see one— but it is very rare that you would, as it is the bluebell painter's job to rise early in the morning and paint blue every new bell that flowered overnight.

Our fairy had an amazing number of bells in the wood to paint, and every day more flowered, but she loved her work, peacefully undertaking the task by painting each flowerhead with gentle brushstrokes and treating each one as if it were a new friend. She was a very talented flower painter and very fast at her work, well; I guess you would have to be to rise through the fairy ranks of flower painters and ascend to bluebells. She was ambitious too: her dream rested on attending the Colour Lantern ball as a fairy dancer.

Oh, how she would love to be there on the stage, but only the very high-ranking fairies had that honour; still, there was always the annual procession to look forward to, and the tournaments and competitions, dancing and music-making, and apple-tree pies for everyone!

All the paint for the flowers was kept in a special oak tree— "special" because it was a very old oak tree, and if you know how trees grow, then you would know that for every year a tree lives its trunk gets wider. This tree was perhaps a thousand years old, and so its trunk was very wide, making it the perfect home for the paint wizards and plenty of storage space to keep the paint needed for all the flowers in the wood.

THE BLUEBELL FAIRY

Every other week, the bluebell fairy would go and collect a large tin of paint. It was quite a long journey, and so she would usually go late afternoon when she had finished that day's painting. This week she was a little later than usual, and she hurried through the wood, darting through the leafy shortcuts and woody, shaded alleys. On arrival at the great oak, she opened the heavy door and climbed the three thousand steps to the paint room.

Indigo, the blue paint wizard, was waiting for her, and he looked very tired, as if he had been working harder than usual. This is very odd, thought the bell fairy, but before she had a chance to ask Indigo why he looked so tired, and why there were more paint tins ready than usual, he told her that she must go and see Spectrum, the head wizard, at once.

This meant climbing another two thousand stairs, for Spectrum's office was right at the top of the oak tree. The fairy had never been up to this office before, and, although she was a little tired, she found her fairylight energy brightening up immediately when faced by this chance to meet the big-colour aura.

Gently she knocked to announce her entrance and turned the big acorn door handle. On entering the room, she was amazed to find there were no walls in Spectrum's office, and from here she could see that the entire forest could be viewed at any time. It wasn't cold or hot either—, the shade and shelter offered by the tree's leaves made perfectly good walls when needed.

Looking at Spectrum, the bluebell fairy saw that his face brightened when he saw her, and his coat started glowing in many different colours, transmitting a wavey rainbow-coloured light into the space around him.

"We are holding the Colour Lantern Ball early this year," he told her. "Infact,

actually we are holding it next Saturday; I know it is not a lot of time, and there are a great deal of preparations to arrange, including painting of all the flowers and the mending of the trees and leaves.

Indigo has mixed up a new batch of paint for the entire bluebell carpet in the wood, and every single flower will need to be repainted with this special shade of blue to be ready for the grand procession next Saturday. Everything must be perfect for this year's Colour Lantern Ball!

Indigo has the paint ready, and you need to take all of it with you today," he finished.

On her way out of Spectrum's office, the little fairy was downhearted, and she felt her energy glow slightly diminish; how could she possibly have all the bells in the forest painted by next Saturday? It was an impossible task! It was a lot of work just to keep up with the daily growth of the new flowers. She went to collect the paint: two hundred large tins were waiting for her from Indigo.

Her glow went to the smallest flicker. How on earth would she manage to move two hundred large tins by herself? she thought. Well, she would just have to go up and down the stairs two hundred times; she did a quick mathematical fairy calculation: two hundred times up and down three thousand stairs— that amounted to over half a million steps! She would fade away at this rate, and, just when she thought she was going to faint, she saw Indigo heading straight towards her; he could see her fairy glow diminishing and was very concerned.

It is not a good thing for a fairy's glow to start to fade, as this is where their special magic comes from— the kind of special magic which is used for flying and vanishing so the fairies don't get seen.

THE BLUEBELL FAIRY

"What troubles you?" he asked her, and when she explained to him that she had only one week to repaint all the old and new bells in the wood, he nodded wisely and produced from under his hat a magic wand.

"This," he said, "is a magic painting wand. All you need to do is dip it into the paint tin, and it will absorb all the paint in that tin; when it has done that, you just need to touch each flowerhead once, and a portion of the paint will transform itself perfectly onto each flower, as if you had painted it with your very own paintbrush; it has the magic to do that only if you are holding it, because you have trained your hands to paint each flower with love and care, and the wand will take that ability from you.

If you rise very early and work very late, you might be able to manage to get the job done. But this you must do, because it is a very important ball this year, I have heard that the colour fairies might be there."

Wow, the colour fairies! thought the little fairy— how she would love to catch a glimpse of one of them. Everyone lived in awe of them; they had the important job of making sure that all the flowers and trees in the world were

THE BLUEBELL FAIRY

always the correct colour and had been painted properly. They were also very wise and trusted with the important knowledge of knowing where colour was kept and how it was made into magic paint.

There was one fairy for each colour, but the most important fairies were known as the Primaries: a pink fairy called Magenta; a blue fairy called Cyan; and a golden fairy who was called Yellow.

These fairies were very beautiful but seldom seen, because they were always very busy, and because of this, quite often they didn't go to the Colour Lantern Ball— but this year they had managed to find time to take a day off, and so Spectrum had decided to go all-out in making sure that the celebrations could take place early to reward them for the work they did.

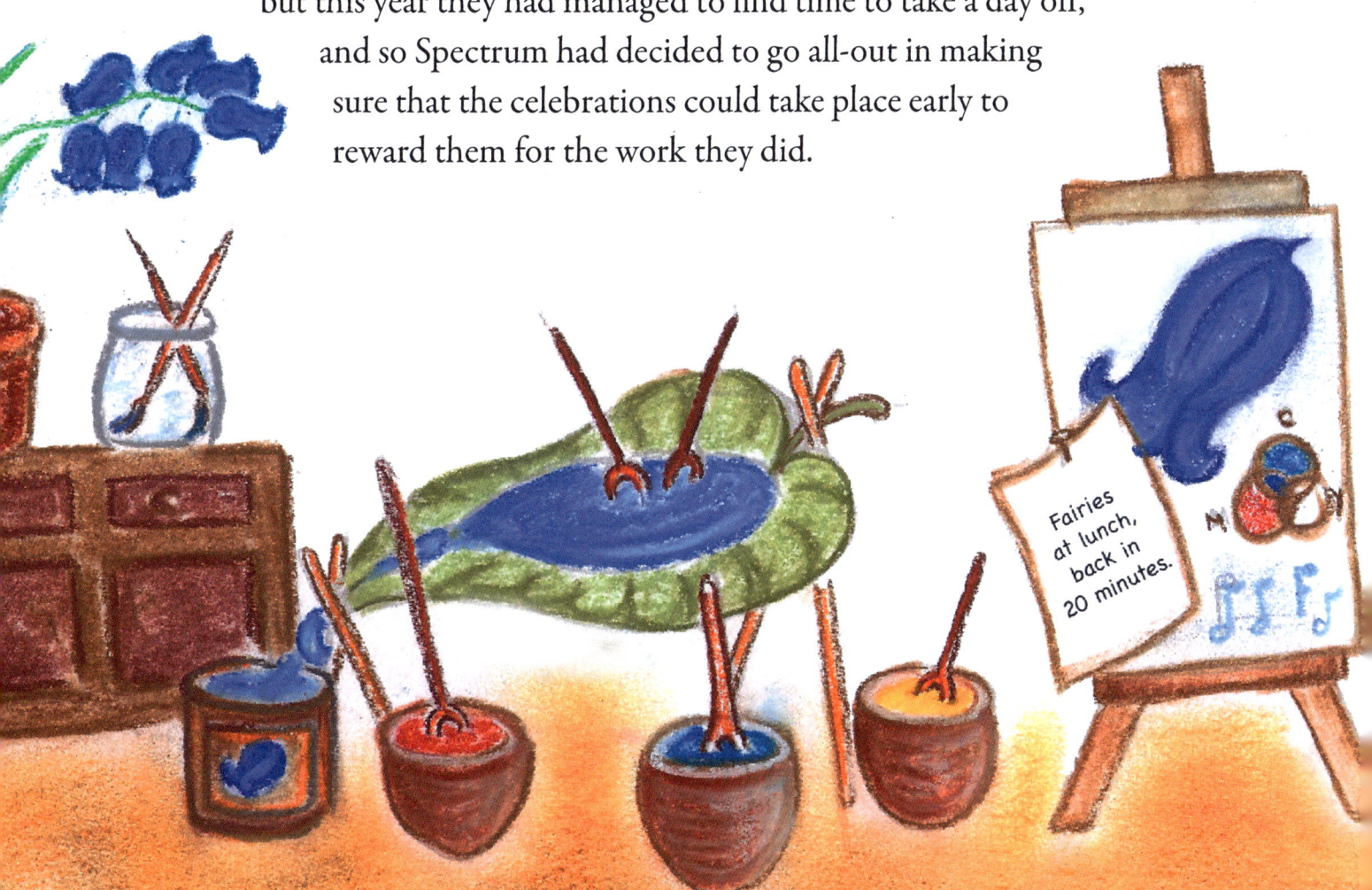

"Now, let's get the paint into the forest," said Indigo. "I will help you," he said, whilst taking off his big hat. "Put each tin of paint into my hat," he said holding it upturned, as if it were a bag.

The little fairy, knowing not to question the wizard, as he obviously had a great deal of magic knowledge, did as he said, but she couldn't help wondering how on earth she would get one large tin of paint into his hat, let alone two hundred.

Still, she did as he said, and, as she dropped the tin into the hat, it became smaller— so small that it was no bigger than the size of a fairy's thimble, which is pretty small, as a fairy is not even as big as a tin of paint. (It is their special powers which gives them amazing strength, which is why the bluebell fairy was able to lift the big tins.)

"Come on," he said. "Let's go and spread the paint tins throughout the forest; if you tell me how many flowers you can paint using one tin, we can line them up along the route of the flowers you need to paint, so just as the wand runs out from the paint of one tin, there will be another tin placed near to the spot that you are in when that happens."

"Thank you, Indigo," said the little fairy when they had finished laying out all the tins of paint through the forest. What a very kind wizard he was, because not all wizards were so helpful to the fairies who worked for them.

"Up early tomorrow, and you will get the job done," said Indigo. Then he disappeared back to the paint room, leaving a puff of magical silver-white and indigo sprinkles in his wake, just as all wizards do when they move from one place to another in an instant.

The next day, just as Indigo had promised, the magic wand painted each flower for her with just one touch, and she managed to get through the carpet of flowers very quickly, but due to the huge amount of bells in the wood, it took a very long time to touch each flower with the magic wand. She had risen early with the dawn and worked right through the day until dusk started to settle, and she could no longer see clearly enough to carry on.

It was a long week of hard work, but by Friday evening she had managed to finish painting every bell flower in the forest, and so off she went to the magic oak tree to let Spectrum know that she had finished the task and to give Indigo back his magic wand.

When she arrived at Spectrum's office, Indigo was already there; he had been sent for when Spectrum had seen from his office that the little fairy was making her way to the large oak tree. Together standing side by side, the colour auras from the two wizards blended, and it was a most remarkable glow that they produced together. The little fairy was in awe of the two magnificent beings, and her mind pictured dreamy images at which she could only marvel: the splendour of the Colour Lantern Ball, when all the paint wizards and colour fairies came together for the special dances; the fairylight, she thought, must be spectacular. Spectrum's voice broke her from the daydream.

"We are very happy that you have managed to finish all the bluebells and are very impressed, but it is a very important day tomorrow, as the colour fairies will be attending the grand procession— and so we want you to keep the wand a little longer and rise early to make sure that any bells that grow overnight are painted before the grand coach leaves the magic oak tree. It will be traveling

through the carpet of bluebells to the ball carrying the colour fairies. Get some good rest tonight, for it is a busy day tomorrow, but you will be able to join the fun in the afternoon and eat apple-tree pies with everyone else.

Well done! I am very impressed with your hard work and flower-painting talent."

Well, with such commendation from Spectrum, the little fairy was positively glowing with pride, so much so that you would have hardly seen her for the bright ball of white light she was projecting. She was so energetic that she didn't know what to do with herself, and so she decided to take a little fairy flight through the wood.

Through the trees and bushes, she flew to the silver lake, where she did a couple of flying somersaults on the lily pads with the frogs who were practicing for the high-leap tournament being held the next day.

After a while she was feeling tired, and so she said her good-byes to the frogs, wished them luck, and went home to bed.

She slept so soundly and so long— too long, infact, after a week of really hard work and the fairyflight she had taken the night before she overslept, and, looking at her dandelion clock, she realised that she had only two hours before the procession started, and she had all the bluebell carpet to check!

THE BLUEBELL FAIRY

She hurried out of her bed attire and put on her best fairy outfit and hoped that she would just not get any flower paint on it; she wouldn't have time to come home and change before the procession began. Tucking the magic wand into her belt, she flew off into the forest.

Carefully checking and painting any new flowers that had bloomed overnight, she had almost finished making sure that every bell flower was blue, when she heard the trumpets of the daffodils sounding in the distance; the grand coach was already on its way.

With the magic wand firmly in her hand, the little fairy flew even faster over the carpet of bluebells to see if any were white. And then she saw it; glowing in the daylight a large crop of white blooms— how could she have missed them, a crop of at least fifty white blooms swaying and not even chiming correctly in tune!

Oh, did I not tell you why the fairies paint the bluebells blue? The special blue paint contains a magical ingredient that makes the bluebells chime in perfect union with one another, so that a beautiful sound is made when the wind gently breezes and forces the bell flowers to sway on the end of their rubbery stalks. It is a beautiful sound that is so soft and gentle that only the magical inhabitants of the forest can hear it. And so the special shade of blue that Indigo had made up for the bluebells to be painted for Saturday's grand procession had contained special musical notes which would give magical instruction, so that the bluebells would chime a new, softer song.

THE BLUEBELL FAIRY

Accompanied by the woodland flutes of the elves, the silver chimes of the gnomes, the drums of the bees, the choruses of the nightingales, and the harps of the leprechauns, the new chime of the bluebells would make a most wonderful melody for the celebrations.

As the grand procession came through the forest, all the inhabitants came out to cheer and look at the colour fairies who were seated inside the majestic coach. And what a coach it was! It had been especially made for the occasion from the reddest and shiniest apple; infact, it was so shiny it would be easy to see your own reflection on its skin, just as if you were looking into a mirror.

At the front of the carriage sat Spectrum, who was giving instruction to the butterfly horses, called butterflorses, who pulled the coach through the air. The aura of the colour fairies inside was so strong that it spilled out of the carriage as the coach travelled onwards, leaving a trail of rainbow dust as it passed by.

Whilst the onlookers were lining up to get a look at the coach and its occupants, our fairy got to work very quickly: one, two, three, four, five, six, seven, she counted to herself, as she tapped each white flower head with the wand. She had just finished, when she turned and saw the majestic fairy coach turning the corner, and so she tucked the wand into the back of her belt and straightened herself up as the coach passed by. As she did so, she saw one last unpainted flower head. Horrified that she had missed it, there was no option. She stood in front of it and hoped that Spectrum wouldn't notice just one white flower. The coach passed by.

THE BLUEBELL FAIRY

Phew! What a relief— but it hadn't passed far when it came to a stop. The primary colour fairies and Spectrum were descending from the coach and heading her way. The little bluebell fairy stepped back closer to the white flower, to avoid it being seen.

"Well done," said Spectrum, "the bluebell carpet looks magnificent, and such a beautiful, beautiful sound the flowers are playing.

It was a lot of hard work to get all these flowers painted in such a short time, but I knew you could do it. The colour fairies are very impressed, and they would like to meet you."

THE BLUEBELL FAIRY

"They would like to meet me?" the bluebell fairy replied in amazement.

"Yes, we would," the colour fairies chorused.

"Infact," said Magenta, the red fairy, "Spectrum has been watching you for us very closely; your dedication and the way you've painted each one of these flowers by hand has impressed us greatly."

The golden fairy, Yellow, then said, "We would like you to join us, and train you as one of the colour fairies. Would you like to become a colour fairy?"

The bluebell fairy was overjoyed, and she had a great flash-of-light aura, but soon she remembered herself, and that it had been the magic wand that she had used to paint each flower and that she hadn't painted each one with her own paintbrush; she was frightened that she could not live up to the colour fairies' expectations.

"I'm afraid I will disappoint you" she said, and, turning to Spectrum she handed him the magic wand from the back of her belt and stood aside from the white flowerhead. "I also missed just this one, and so, you see, I am not that impressive after all."

Spectrum sighed and looked down on her; his expression was sad. Sad, because he could feel the little fairy's disappointment in herself, and because she had worked so hard, and still she did not feel her own magic.

Spectrum then smiled fondly at her and said, "When you touched each flowerhead with the wand, Indigo told you that the magic wand would take the ability to apply the paint from you, just as if you were

painting each one individually with your own paintbrush. The wand did not have that power within it; you gave that power to the wand; the wand was just to help carry all that paint easily, so you could fly over the carpet and get the job done in the very short time that you had to repaint each flower.

You don't need that wand anymore. The magic needed to paint the flowers came from inside you; you have developed this power by working so hard and painting so many flowers in your fairy life with love and dedication. That magic is all your own, and you are a very precious fairy."

Then Cyan, the blue fairy, said "Touch the white flowerhead with your hand, and see what happens."

The bluebell fairy did this, and the flower changed colour: it became blue. "But how did that happen?" she said. "Where did the blue paint come from?"

Magenta stepped forward and said, "To be able to paint every flower the same colour is also very special; you never tire of the colour blue, you never complain, and you never become bored, and, because of this, every time you painted a flower blue, your aura soaked up any extra paint that was not needed from each flower.

You can now create blue just by touching an object and desiring it to be that colour. Your love of blue is that strong. I love red, I can create red, and I have that power within me, just as you have the power to create blue."

"It is a very rare gift," said Yellow, the golden fairy. "It can only be developed through love. Some fairies will paint all their lives but never be able to create colour from their auras instead of with a paintbrush. They love their work— we don't doubt that— and they are also very special, because it takes a lot of love and dedication to the forest to do this every day."

THE BLUEBELL FAIRY

"But what you have," interjected Cyan, "is a very rare gift— a pure love of just one colour, so much that you are actually able to create it— and because of this we would like you to join us and let us show you how to use that gift and develop this new magic you now have."

"It is a dream come true," said the bluebell fairy, and her energy intensified so much that her aura glowed so brightly that a most remarkable thing happened: her aura of white light started flickering, and with each flicker it started to change colour; with each flicker a blue light started to appear, and then, as the flickering got stronger and stronger, so did the blue light that she was projecting.

Soon the flickering stopped, and her aura became a beautiful soft violet blue, and the honour of this name they bestowed on her. She would be known as the colour fairy Violetblue. She would be given the chance to develop her new found magical power to create this colour for the paint needed for bluebells, hyacinths, irises, violets, and just about any violet blue flowers you've ever seen.

"Wow! What a magnificent sight!" the onlookers said, as they witnessed the transformation and birth of a new colour fairy. They would remember this special day for a long time to come.

It was a dream come true for the little fairy; could her day get any better after she had had such a sleepy start? Of course it could! After all, she lived in a world of woodland enchantment, a world in which she would be attending the Colour Lantern Ball and arriving there in the ruby red coach as one of the colour fairies herself.

THE END

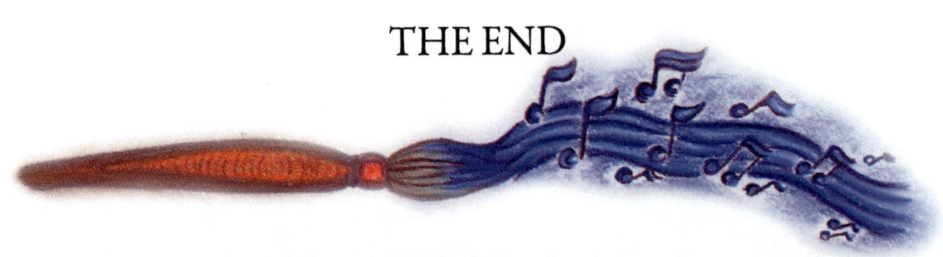

WHAT ABOUT YOU...

If you lived in an enchanted woodland, what job would you like to do?

Would you be a flower painter, a musicial elf, a cook mouse, a tree mender, or a fairy dancer? Perhaps you would like to be a wizard?

What magical talent would you choose to have?

The Bluebell fairy nearly fainted when she calculated how many times she would have to go up and down the steps carrying tins of paint, until Indigo helped her to take the paint into the wood. Do you remember how many steps she would of had to take?

Can you recite or sing a times table?

What is your favourite flower or plant?
Where does is grow? Can you draw it here?

If you could make a magical song what instrument would you use to play it?

What is your favourite song?

The Bluebell fairy's favourite colour is blue, especially violetblue, the colour she is named after.

What is your favourite colour?
Why? What do you like about it most?
Where do you see it most often?

FROM THE AUTHOR

One night many years ago, my niece Aimee, who was seven at the time, asked me to tell her a bedtime story, and suddenly being put on the spot, I created "The Bluebell Fairy." The very next evening Aimee asked me to retell her the story, and the parts that I had forgotten she promptly corrected and filled in for me. It was this that made me realise that my simple story had captured her imagination, and that it was a story worth giving to the children of the world.

The stories I write are to inspire the imaginations of children to see beyond the walls of the world and appreciate the natural spirit that is around them. I hope the illustrations will capture their attention and invoke them to live a life of colour, unafraid of becoming their best possible selves and achieving what they want with their lives. The stories are intended to be read to a child, to create magic for healthy bedtime dreams and to leave parent and child in loving, reflective states.

With that thought in mind, I give you one magical wish of my own: may a child's laughter live long in your ears, well after the belly aching stops, may chalk drawings continue to adorn our pavements and daisy chains continue to adorn our adult heads, and may images of poppy dollies and fuchsia ballerinas dance in your mind's eye when you lock down your eyelids for the night.

With love and fairy sprinkles on you all, x

Michelle.

Other books by Michelle A. Soden-Gilkes

Do You Believe In Magic?
The Bluebell Fairy and other tales of woodland enchantment

If you enjoyed this book discover more about the Bluebell Fairy's home from other magical stories about the Wizzoes and Pixies that live there.

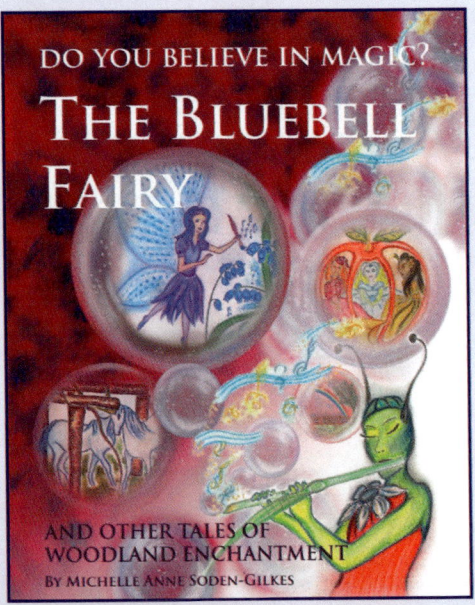

www.TheBluebellFairy.com

Magic The Moon Bear: A Birthday Adventure

The first book in the Magic The Moon Bear series. Magic journeys to Earth to celebrate his 100th birthday.

Printed in Great Britain
by Amazon